# THE LORE OF RAMRIDGE

# THE LORE OF RAMRIDGE

Book One of The Lore of Ramridge Series

## KARUNA SAVOIE

Illustrations By
**KARUNA SAVOIE**

Library of Congress Control Number
2018955454

ISBN: 978-1-7323192-2-6 (ebook)
ISBN: 978-1-7323192-5-7 (pbk.)

First Edition, 2018

*For my parents*

# CHAPTER ONE

JAMES HAD RUN AWAY for the best of reasons.

The sky was the brilliant color of ice, the air was laced with the scent of woodsmoke—and James was bored. It was the perfect day for a trip to Ramridge Ranch. The family-fun farm had been Frumentville's only source of excitement for years. The pumpkin carving and marshmallow roasting had been defining parts of James's childhood.

But that had all ended when a rumor began spreading—kids were going missing in the ranch's corn maze. Of course, his mother not only believed it, but established what James thought was the *stupidest* rule. For his own safety, James was no longer allowed to go to Ramridge Ranch at all.

It had been a whole year since his last visit, and a year was too long.

James left his skateboard in the near-empty parking lot and sprinted into the barn. He located the admission table. Digging his hand into his back pocket, he dug out a couple of crumpled bills. In one swift motion the young woman behind the table took the money and whipped a wristband from the box.

James checked the time on the wall—just a little past four. He had told his mother that he would be at Logan's house for a few hours. He could skateboard back in time for dinner.

*But she'd kill me if she knew I was here,* James thought as he dashed around to the open barn doors.

It was bad enough that school was boring. Worse, that his best friend, Logan, wouldn't stop bragging about her weekends spent playing manhunt at the ranch. Even worse, the rumor had been the main topic in the sixth grade for weeks—his classmates wouldn't stop talking about it! Hearing the stories made James just itch to witness the scene.

James craved the excitement of seeing the place for himself, and even thought that a bit of fear every once in a while never hurt anyone. In fact, fear was essential to an adventurous life, and an adventurous life was one of James's main goals.

Taking matters into his own hands was just the next natural step.

"Finally," James exhaled, bursting out of the barn doors and into the silvery light of the day. He stopped short to take in the view of the farm. As he squinted out into the landscape, his smile faded, and a slight chill edged beneath his skin. "Uh ..."

*This place changed.*

An uncanny sensation twisted his gut. He had the desire to turn back, declare his adventure paused for the time being. But his gaze locked on the distant, swaying fronds of the corn maze. Logan's voice echoed through his head.

*You haven't lived 'till you've gone back into the maze,* she had told James, when they were in a particularly boring lesson about times tables. James had laughed at her next words. *I swear, it felt like someone was following us the whole time! It was* crazy.

"That's it," James declared. He began marching down the path. "I'm going, I'm going, I'm going."

## CHAPTER TWO

PARKER WRIGHT WAS up and about long before the roosters of Ramridge signaled the start of the work day.

The man never disrupted the precious routine of his morning. As soon as he arose, Parker draped his woolen robe around his shoulders, pulled on his socks, and reached for his battered straw hat. He waddled over to the refrigerator to locate the hefty jug of cider and poured himself a short glass. He swallowed his heart medicine pill, ignoring the one prescribed by his physician to improve his mood.

Over the years, Gracie had hounded him to follow the doctor's orders. Finding the pill box full and sealed in plastic on the countertop, she confronted him and his typical stubborn attitude. In return, Parker said, "There ain't nothin' the matter with my nervous system. Besides, anybody who's got a big business to manage is likely to have a temper sometimes."

Parker ran the ranch, but Gracie ran Parker.

The old man clambered down the creaky set of steps to the main floor of the barn. Pushing the wide double doors open, he greeted Ramridge Ranch with a wheezing cough. He surveyed the morning light plunging into the valley of corn and the early morning dew that speckled the grazing field. Parker drank in the sight, the perfect calm of the late dawn, the suspense before the raucous hours of work.

As soon as he could tear himself away from the view, the old farmer was ready for his breakfast of four heavily-peppered scrambled eggs, toast smeared with apple butter and another glass of cider. He returned to the kitchen with his appetite whet. As usual, Gracie was awake, dutifully knitting the Christmas sweaters her grandchildren would never wear, unless they were actually in her presence.

*The Frument Review* lay on the kitchen table and caught Parker's eye. He grimaced at the headline.

"LOCAL RANCH LOSES ANOTHER YOUNG VISITOR?"

Parker spat out the window, placing the cigar down on a tarnished ashtray.

"Darn this town," he sputtered. "There's nothin' the matter with my farm."

The last thing he needed was for *The Frument*

*Review* to feed into the gossip. Over the past year, the spreading rumors had caused visitor numbers to drop. With this story in the paper, numbers were likely to drop even more. If they did, he would be in trouble.

With a grunt, Parker frowned down at the article before clenching it in a calloused fist. With effort, he pushed himself out of the wooden chair and shuffled over to the cooling fireplace beside the ironing board.

He tossed in the newspaper.

Gracie Wright, round-faced and hunch-backed, put down her knitting and picked up her cane. A sturdy woman for her age, she wore a wide blazer, a long, flower-print skirt and a pair of rough black work boots. Both the top and bottom of her wooden cane were carved in such a way that it appeared as if ears of corn were sprouting from the very wood itself.

Gracie took a look at her husband, then at the fire-place. She let out a long, shaky breath.

"Parker," she said. The old man squinted at her. "You can't just keep ignoring a newspaper article because you don't like what it reads."

Parker sneered, resting his hand on the stone counter-top. "Them reporters got nothin' better to do."

"You're being childish." The old woman pushed herself out of the chair with the help of her cane. Then, resting her cane against the countertop, she turned on the stove. A twitching ring of blue formed beneath the metal bars. "You know, Parker, the landlord called again this morning."

"Again?" Parker wiped an arm across his forehead, letting out a rugged sigh. "Jesus, Gracie. What'd he say?"

"Same thing he said last week." She set a kettle to boil. "Parker, whether you believe that headline or not, it's no lie that Ramridge's profits have plummeted. If we don't do something fast—"

"I know, Gracie," Parker mumbled. Shaking his head, he plopped himself down into the armchair, and his weight sunk deep into the cushions. "We'll lose profit," he repeated.

"*No...*" Raising an eyebrow, Gracie turned to face her husband. She lowered her voice to a stark whisper. "More than that. You'll lose your job, Parker. We'll lose our home. We could lose *everything.*"

Muttering under his breath, Parker rubbed his face with the heels of his calloused hands. "I've been doing everything I can to fix this, Gracie." He gave a guttural sigh. "But one year goes by quick as autumn herself. And I've done everything."

"Except for one thing," Gracie said. The kettle began hissing, steam undulating around the compact room. After flicking the dial to turn off the heat, the old woman batted her hand back and forth over the kettle to clear the air. "You've been taking this all on by yourself. I know you, Parker—and I know you like your individualism. But you need help with this."

"I have you," Parker coughed, giving his wife an impish grin. Gracie smiled, shaking her head. After a moment, Parker continued, "You know, Gracie, people gotta quit badgering me about my farm."

Gracie paused in pouring the hot water. "Here we go again, Parker!"

"I'm telling ya, Gracie," he said, raising his voice, "whenever Halloween rolls around, this town goes *nuts* coming up with these stories—and they don't stop!" He shook his head and adjusted the buckle on his wide, braided belt. "Nothin' wrong with my farm. It's just a rumor."

Gracie turned to face him, prepared to lecture once again. But the newspaper lying crumpled in the fireplace caught her eye. "Well..." She nodded to it. "What *does* it read?"

The old man began muttering under his breath. Placing her hands on her hips, she stepped toward him. "Parker?"

The farmer gazed down at his boots.

"Parker," she said sternly.

He ground his teeth.

Gracie walked over to the fireplace, reached for the crumpled newspaper, and hobbled over to her husband. "You! Old man!" she commanded, whipping Parker in the stomach with the paper. A bit of chipped teeth showed through her half snarl, half frown. "Look up at your wife!"

Parker locked eyes with her. He couldn't help but chuckle.

"Parker, this is the third time some unfortunate child went missing. And each time, even after the harvest, after our workers *and* the police scan the whole place, there's never a sign of 'em," Gracie said.

She paused to flatten out the newspaper before continuing.

"Parker, people are getting spooked—you can't blame them! And if you don't want your farm *and* our lives to turn to ashes, I suggest you accept the situation. Because *that*—" Gracie pointed to the fireplace, "—is not what the ranch needs."

Parker sat there for a moment, slack-jawed, staring at his wife. "But, Gracie, don't 'cha remember when that other poor child went missin' decades back?"

"I've certainly *heard* of it, Parker." Gracie squinted down at her husband. "But we hadn't even moved up here at the time."

"That's just it," Parker blurted, jabbing a finger toward the ceiling. "This town is paranoid, Gracie. They make this stuff up. Once, some little girl went missin' in the valley. Then another went missin'. Then another. They go 'round conspirin', but they haven't found a darned thing to prove any of it. And now, they're puttin' the blame on *us*, Gracie!"

Gracie shoved the paper back into Parker's hands. Shuffling back to the counter, she grabbed her cane.

"As much as you deny it, if children *are* going missing, their parents must be worried *sick!*" The floorboards wheezed beneath her stride as the cane knocked into the old, flimsy wood. Gracie stopped at the end of the counter. Before reaching for their stash of tea bags, she shook her cane back at her husband. "You need to stop whining about *The Review*, and start taking control of this mess! It's for your own good."

"Fine, Gracie." After a contemplative moment, Parker groaned and wiped the back of his neck in defeat. "But what am I supposed to do about this?"

"Call Hall."

Gracie said it a little too matter-of-factly for Parker's liking. He responded with a harrumph.

"He'll bring all his deputies. They'll search the farm. Then we'll know for sure that what the town's saying isn't true. *The Frument Review* can print a story about *that!*"

Parker pushed himself out of the armchair and trudged back over to the window. He squinted out at the endless waves of corn. "It'll take 'em weeks to rake through the maze. I could get it done faster myself."

With her cane, Gracie went over to the window to stand beside Parker. "Here, dear." Gracie firmly held the mug out in front of Parker's clutched hands. Without moving his eyes from the view, Parker took the steaming mug from her hands, and took a large, scalding slurp. Gracie nodded in approval, following his gaze out the window.

"Well, if you do *something*," she continued, "people will stop telling tales. Call Hall."

"All right," Parker mumbled, the hot tea softening his thoughts. "Let's give it one more day. I'll get in contact with the sheriff tomorrow. Shut down the ranch. Get things straightened out. But I'm tellin' ya, Gracie, there ain't a thing in Ramridge Ranch that gets past me. I've been runnin' this place for years, and I've seen *nothin'*— not a piece of straw or a pumpkin seed out of place. Not a darned thing. And I'm gonna prove to this town that the same goes with my maze."

## CHAPTER THREE

AFTER DARK, when he was certain the old caretakers were holed up under their bedcovers and security had made a final sweep of the maze, Conner emerged from the corn.

He slunk out from deep in the patch of stalks, oblivious to the scrapes the thick leaves made on his skin. With his knife in one hand, a coil of rope over his shoulder and wooden posts under his arm, he lumbered down the dried dirt pathway. Cryptic shadows formed spikes between his footsteps.

Conner inhaled the crisp fragrance of corn and the scent of smoke the wind carried from remnants of the bonfire. He took in the quiet emptiness of the night and the reflective light of his blade.

He soon reached the entrance to the maze. The broad wooden sign creaked in the breeze. Conner went right to work—setting down his knife and rope, he pounded the three wooden posts into the earth in a close-knit line. Then he paused, sticking his fingers through his long, matted beard. The posts were as tall as his shoulders, and thick enough to hold a sack of potatoes.

Conner pressed his lips into a jagged grin.

He held one end of the rope to a post, tied it around the top and held it out taut before him. Lifting the knife, he began to sever the rope into three equal pieces. Again, he paused to review his next course of action. Stuffing his hand into the back pocket of his beaten jeans, Conner stepped back to view his creation.

Suddenly, he felt a jab in his palm.

"Yow!" Conner wailed, whipping his hand out of his pocket. Then slowly, he reached back into it to pull out a sewing needle. With a grunt, Conner dropped it to the ground.

Quickly, he tied the pieces of rope to the other two posts—and his work was complete. Sucking on the cut in his palm, Conner trudged into the shadows, back into the swaying wall of corn.

---

PARKER LIT A CIGAR, put it to his chapped lips and slowly inhaled the smoke. The month of October was just reaching its peak, but frost was already settling in the Huron Mountains. It cast a ghostly shadow over the valley. With the ranch closed, the usual bustle of workers setting up for the day's events was replaced by silence.

The morning was still, and eerie.

*Might as well be a ghost farm,* he grumbled in his head, *to go with this good-for-nothin' ghost town.*

The old man turned his attention to the quivering wall of corn in the distance. The dense, loping corn maze washed through the valley of Ramridge and skipped into perfect pleats of bronze in the ancient foothills. It never ceased to amaze him, and yet, today it did not bring him the usual joy.

The maze was Parker's pride and glory. It had been his idea, after all. Since its creation, tourists had flocked to Frumentville from all over the county—Ramridge's maze was the biggest attraction.

*Not anymore,* Parker thought, thinking back to the newspaper headline. *Last year, things were different.*

He blew a cloud of smoke out into the already dusky landscape. He moved his eyes along it. Where once there were parties with marshmallows sizzling under garnishing stripes of caramel was now a cold fire pit. Where visitors once gathered around the tree stump podium to sit under the stars, there was silence.

Today, Parker's unbreakable routine was destined to falter for the very first time. After breakfast, he made his way to the children's petting pen a few yards away from the corn maze. Parker began his rounds. But as he was feeding the sheep, Parker Junior, his daily pound of corn and oats, he spotted something out of the ordinary near the entrance to the maze.

Three wooden posts poked their way out of the ground. Each post had a short rope tied to the top of it, and scraps of straw were littered about their bases. The eggs he had just eaten felt as if they were moving in his stomach. Parker had never noticed the posts there before —it was as if they had materialized overnight.

Upon drawing closer for inspection and crouching down as far as his rickety knees would allow, he spied a sewing needle within a clump of grass. Parker shook his head.

Materialize overnight? It was an absurd idea. There was nothing odd about three wooden posts and a sewing needle.

Was there?

"Must've fallen out of Gracie's sewin' basket." Parker shrugged, wondering why his wife would ever bring her sewing anywhere near the smelly goat pen and trying to ignore the posts altogether.

He fed the trio of goats—Blackie, Bleater and Phoebe —and made a mental note to turn them loose to the pasture by midafternoon. Parker placed the bucket of dry food on a flower barrel and turned to amble up the dirt pathway.

By the time he reached the barn, the farmer had thought enough about the wooden posts and the needle. They pricked at his nerves. After all, Parker had not lied when he said that he would never let even a piece of straw or a pumpkin seed escape his notice.

Once Parker reached the entrance, he spotted the ancient metal phone hanging from a spiraling cord in the wall. Not relishing his task, he lifted the receiver to his ear, stuck a finger into the rotary and dialed the sheriff's number. A long, piercing ring split the peaceful silence. The phone rang three more times before the sheriff finally picked up, mumbling a greeting from the other end of the line.

"Morning, Hall," Parker spoke into the receiver. "It's Parker Wright."

There was excited chatter from the other end, a rushed sequence of "How's"—"How do you do?," "How's Gracie?," "How's the ranch?," "How's this year's pickin's?" It had been quite some time since they had last spoken.

"We have a concern," Parker finally had the chance to say. "Somethin' with my maze, or somethin'."

Sheriff Hall told him that he had, indeed, been receiving calls from not only a paranoid parent, but from *The Frument Review*. Another child gone missing in the vast corn maze—one more reason for parents to shun the ranch, as much as their children begged to return.

"Doesn't sound like any credible calls to me," Parker mumbled under his breath. But the sheriff, with his keen ears, heard it anyway.

"Forget about the newspaper, Parker," Sheriff Hall

continued. "A mother called me yesterday, earlier this morning and just a few *minutes* ago. She's sure her son is lost, and I've been investigating the situation, but—"

"Tell ya what," Parker said into the receiver. "I haven't found a single trace of nothin' in my corn maze, let alone a kid or whatever people are ravin' about. But, Sheriff, if you can come on down to the ranch and take a look for yourself, please, be my guest. I need ya to clear the ranch's name, once and for all."

# CHAPTER FOUR

THE PARK, Conner reckoned, was closed.

Around this time of the season, people should have been flocking to the ranch for the year's last rounds of fun and games. But there hadn't been a single visitor to his maze in a while—until now.

*The maze,* Conner reminded himself. *The maze is what should be bringing 'em.*

He chuckled to himself, squinting up at the clear sky. Above him, columns of corn glinted gold in the light as they swayed left and right in the wind. Conner felt the sunlight warm his leathery forehead, and stuck out his tongue to catch a taste of the sweet air.

Then, resuming his solemn expression, he turned back to his newest save.

"So," he croaked, gesturing to the shaking boy huddled in his fleece. "How do you like my maze?"

The boy's ankles and wrists were bound by a ratty, old rope. Upon looking at Conner, as close as he could, he drew up his legs to his chest, silently cursing the rope that bound him. Conner's lips cracked into a smile, showing an array of yellow teeth stained from years of chewing on kernels.

The boy, shivering, glanced up at him.

"Please, sir," he said. "I need to go find my momma." His once wavy tufts of hair flattened against his eyes as a breeze picked up.

Conner snarled, bending down on one knee. The boy opened his eyes wider, but seeing Conner's vile expression, shut them tightly again.

"Please?" he repeated, this time through his clenched jaw.

Conner raised his eyebrows. "What's yer name, kid?"

The boy buried his face inside the sleeve of his fleece, only to mutter an inaudible curse. Conner cleared his throat—a large, frightening sound that made the boy cringe and forced him to look into the man's eyes.

"James," he squeaked. "But my momma told me never to talk to strangers."

"James!" A quiver crept across Conner's lips. He held out a dirty, calloused hand. "Welcome home."

James warily reached out his tied hands to shake Conner's, then quickly pulled them back. He glanced around the small clearing in the corn patch. *There's gotta be an exit somewhere.* James had been stuck with the creepy old grandpa for a couple nights. But it had felt like a week.

*Hungry. Tired. Hungry. Tired.*

Conner emitted another revolting grunt and spat into the corn. James clutched his stomach. He felt sick. He needed to run, to get out of here, but his legs were tied.

James didn't know how much longer he could pull off his little boy act. Even though the strange man had done nothing but ramble on about his beloved maze, James's terror was growing. He had thought if he acted young and scared, the old man might take pity on him—perhaps even let him go.

But it was useless. James could not stop trembling. He wanted to find an escape.

*Needed* to.

"How old are you, James?"

Squinting up at the man again, the boy grimaced.

"Twelve," James peeped. His skin turned cold. He could have lied about his age. His sister always said he looked quite young for his grade level, but the word had slipped out. Suddenly, he flushed with irritation. "But why do *you* need to know that, you creep?"

Conner sneered at him. "You're trouble," he said gruffly. "That's what you are, you spiteful thing. Didn't your momma ever teach you manners?"

James did not budge. "Get me outta here," he hissed. Then, James thought of something else. "If you don't," he continued hesitantly, "the whole sheriff's department will be looking for me."

*But what if they don't?* James thought, and swallowed. *No one knows where I am.*

As far as he knew, nothing bad ever happened in Frumentville. He had never seen the police force ever show up for anything. The most trouble anyone had ever caused was making a few cheeky prank calls—something his friend, Logan, may or may not have been involved in.

*Does Frumentville even* have *a police department?* James sighed. *Of course they do. They have to.*

Conner shook his head, running a hand through his rugged beard. "Sure," he scoffed. "Just like they did for the others. You keep believin' that, James."

James raised an eyebrow. He felt a lump in his throat. *The others?*

"Why don't ya tell me why ya ran away, anyhow? There's gotta be a good reason for it," Conner persisted. The two of them had gone through the same conversation the hour before, and the hour before that, and the hour before *that*. Still, James could not figure out what the man was talking about.

All James remembered was running through the maze. Then, out of nowhere, he was forced into the wall of corn as if a lion were dragging him into its lair. The next thing he knew, he was being interrogated by his captor—the same question, over and over again.

"I'm telling you, I'm not a runaway," James said, exasperated. "Who are you, anyway? Why'd you take me?"

*And why are you living in a stinkin' pile of corn?* he wanted to ask him, but he held off.

Conner straightened his back, tilting his head up to the billowing corn leaves. "Once, I was a runaway, too," he murmured. James rolled his eyes. "And when I found this place, I thought I landed in escapee heaven." Conner was unaware that the boy was hardly listening—and hardly cared, for that matter. "The maze is my home. The maze is what bringed me here. The maze is everything to me, James."

James glanced up at the hulking figure, narrowing his eyes. Conner's voice dropped to a low, stark whisper.

"Everything, James," Conner wheezed. "Everything."

## CHAPTER FIVE

"Let's get to the bottom of this, shall we?"

Sheriff Hall planted a big, crooked grin on his face before slamming the truck door shut. Winking at Parker, he sauntered down the path that led to the maze as if he had done it countless times, leaving the farmer to catch up with him.

"So, what is it you seen, Wright?" Hall asked again.

"I tol' you, Sheriff—these suspicious-lookin' wooden posts out there yonder. I didn't put 'em there," he repeated for the third time, gesturing to the entrance.

Once they reached the maze, Sheriff Hall inspected the posts with an intense, squinting gaze, and furrowed his brow. The wooden posts, sure enough, stood ominously amongst the random scraps of rope. "Might be worth investigating," he said.

The sheriff circled one of the posts and tugged at its rope. He stooped down and lifted a piece of orange thread between his fingers, and nonchalantly tucked it into the breast pocket of his leather vest. He stood and nodded at Parker, who widened his eyes in anticipation.

"I can't reckon what this means, Wright." Sheriff Hall sniffed, lifting his chin. He reached his hand up to pet his mustache. "But it looks like three wooden posts."

"I know darn right it's three wooden posts, Hall," Parker grumbled, his volume rising. "What I need to know is who put 'em here, and why. 'Cause I certainly did not put 'em here."

"Calm yourself, old man." Sheriff Hall rested his hands on his hips, where his belt sagged from the weight of an ornate turquoise buckle. "Let me investigate. You know how to navigate this maze, don't ya? Because I don't wanna get trapped in there by myself! Lots o' twists an' turns in there, am I right?"

"Sure, I can navigate," Parker said, straightening his posture. "Whatever ya need for your investigation. I just want to get to the bottom of this as fast as possible. I don't want these nosy townsfolk whisperin' behind my back any longer."

"Let's get to it then, Parker." Sheriff Hall straightened his hat and laid a hand on his belt as he sauntered into the entrance of the maze.

"Say, Hall." Parker hurried his steps. "What's all the

commotion about my maze, anyhow? I wanna hear your thoughts on it."

"Commotion?"

*The Frument Review* headline flashed before Parker's eyes. "The town thinks some kid got lost in it. That's why you're here, Sheriff—to prove 'em wrong."

"Whoa there, old man." The sheriff laid a hand on Parker's shoulder. "Prove 'em wrong? I'm just here to investigate the situation. *Then* we'll see about proving."

"That's just—" Parker's boot snagged a nest of dead corn leaves and mud, and he almost tripped right into the sheriff. The farmer thought he knew his maze well enough, despite having never set foot past the entrance sign. He had drawn the design himself—but it was the workers who cut it. The falter in his steps gave him a jolt. "Darn path. How do these kids do it?"

The sheriff raised an eyebrow. "They're smaller, I guess. What was it you were trying to say?"

Parker jumped as the leaves from a corn stalk brushed against his shoulder. "Ah, what was I ... oh, yes. That's the thing, all these investigations. Didn't your deputies already come lookin' through my farm?"

"No, I don't suppose they did, Wright. Anyway, the case for those missing kids was closed. They were runaways."

"Runaways," Parker muttered. "So, what's with the town being obsessed with Ramridge Ranch, then? If they never proved they disappeared from here, ain't this just another runaway?"

Sheriff Hall stayed silent, slowing his pace as he reached up to pat his breast pocket. "I guess we'll see about that, Wright."

Unsatisfied, Parker peeked back over his shoulder once, twice, then three times, looking at the tops of the three posts through the foliage. He felt as if they were staring right back at him.

———

Conner sniffed, then whipped his head to the side, lips curling into a snarl.

"Someone's coming."

"I told you they would co—"

Conner yanked James up from the ground by the collar of his fleece and began dragging him through the stalks. James had been waiting for this moment, however, and was not about to let the man wrestle him away to another hidden corner of the maze.

James began screaming. His harsh, raspy voice punctured the air and stung Conner's eardrums. "Help! Someone, help! Anyone!"

"Shut up. You don't want 'em to catch ya, now do ya?"

James ignored him, continuing to writhe and shriek in Conner's grasp as the older man clamped a scabbed hand over his mouth. The scent of Conner's palm made James retch in disgust.

"Help!" he shouted. The slashing of corn leaves against his skin burned like cuts he had received from slipping off his skateboard onto pavement. He continued weakly kicking and wriggling to loosen Conner's grip. But with his feet and hands tied, he had no luck.

*I'm not gonna die out here.* James tried breaking the rope that bound his wrists. *I can't die out here.*

Suddenly, Conner shifted his hand from James's mouth. Before James could let out another scream, Conner stuffed a wad of corn leaves between the boy's teeth. James widened his eyes and choked on the sharp leaves. Moaning, he continued to flail his body as Conner hauled him off, his feet snagging in clumps of roots and leaves. In the distance, he heard a muffled crunching through the leaves. The sound slowly diminished.

James's hopes of freedom crumbled with each second that passed.

"I hope you're happy," Conner sneered. "You almost got us caught. Do you know how hard it is to stay hided out 'ere? No. I guess ya just need to be taught a thing or two."

James wanted to protest, but he could only shut his eyes and hope that whoever else was out in the maze was searching for him.

He prayed.

"Open your eyes," Conner commanded as he pulled

the slobbery leaves from the boy's mouth. He swayed to a stop. "There's a plank here that ya don't wanna trip on."

James's eyes were near slits as he wearily opened them. He began coughing and hacking his throat to rid his mouth of the taste of corn leaves. Just as he glanced up at his new surroundings, Conner pushed him into a dark room. James fell to his knees and wiped the drool from his chin.

"What is this place?" James asked hoarsely, lifting his heavy gaze into the dimness.

He was in some sort of shack.

His eyes strained. Dirt, hay bales and even pieces of paper were strewn across the wooden floor. The only light was provided by the opened door and a small window with boards nailed across it.

James considered escaping out of the window. He began looking around, searching for something to break the boards with. Tacked on one wall, a narrow shelf was adorned with hooks, drab bundles of thread, a chipped drinking glass filled with tarnished sewing needles and a couple of crusty, stained handkerchiefs.

He gazed back at the window. His hope sank.

*Forget it. It's just too small for me to fit through.*

"This is my home, James—the heart of the maze. And it's where you'll be kept safe with them others," Conner answered, his voice lifting. "Them others can be shy, so I thought I'd wait a bit before I brought ya."

James's eyes drifted across the cramped, shadow-filled space. "Others?" he repeated tonelessly. The word stuck in his thoughts, though its meaning left him. He could think of little else but his own much-needed escape.

*Please,* James prayed, *just let me go!*

He felt a sudden heated tremor. Hatred. It ebbed as quickly as it came, but left James furious—at himself.

*I'm so stupid,* he seethed silently. Tears lined his eyelashes. *Why did I come here? What if I never escape?*

"Look, James—this here's Harry and Violet," Conner said proudly, spinning James toward the back of the shed.

Amongst the shadows, the boy made out two small faces.

"It's another runaway," Conner said. "Don't be shy. Come on out, show yerselves."

James narrowed his eyes as slowly, very slowly, the two figures emerged from the shadows. A boy and a girl, appearing to be the same age as James.

He shuddered.

The girl, Violet, had messy red bangs that swept away from her eyes. The rest of her hair was pulled back in a short ponytail. She clung to a patched blanket, and James noticed the Ramridge Ranch entrance band still hung around her frail wrist, the logo long worn off.

He shifted his gaze to the boy, Harry. His curly brown hair was tangled with clumps of dried mud and pieces of corn leaves, his overalls ragged and torn. Harry's gaze was blank, strangely vacant, as if he didn't see James at all.

James bit his lip as his eyes began studying the children's limbs. As far as he could tell, they weren't constrained by rope like he was. He glanced over his shoulder and caught a glimpse of a large lock hooked to the outside of the door. Shivering, he turned back to the children.

Conner had locked the children in.

But for how long?

James's hands began to quiver at the thought. The rope binding his ankles suddenly had the weight of an iron chain.

James turned his focus back to Harry and Violet. Squinting closer, he spotted something peculiar, besides their tattered clothes and dirt-stained cheekbones. It writhed in their expressions, boiled behind their eyes. Were there slivers of sound barred from behind their quivering lips?

Or only silence?

James didn't want to believe that what he saw was real—a line of blood trickling down Violet's jaw, a cross-hatch of thread binding Harry's pale lips shut. It had to be a figment of the shadows.

Was he hallucinating?

"No way," James whispered, stunned, backing away from the children. A tremor passed through his body—a dose of pure, invasive fear. "This isn't real. This is ... *insanity*."

He bumped into Conner, who grabbed James's shoulder. James let out a hideous cry as he whipped around to face a freshly threaded needle.

A pale orange thread glinted between Conner's dirt-clotted fingernails.

# CHAPTER SIX

"How 'bout we start on the perimeter of the maze, and work our way to the center?" Sheriff Hall said, motioning with his hands. "Whaddaya say, Wright?"

"Fine, Hall. That's just fine," Parker grumbled as he stepped on a rotted half of a corn cob. He raised a fist into the air. "This corn ain't for you, you slobbering bird-brains!"

Sheriff Hall scratched his beard as they turned a corner. "Maybe you should consider gettin' some scare-crows, Wright. My in-laws—they own a cute little potato farm down in Pennsylvania—used some of those potato sacks and some old trousers and put up a few of 'em scarecrows. Haven't seen a single slobbering varmint ever since."

"Isn't that fine," Parker grumbled again, kicking aside

a patch of uprooted weeds. "Say, Hall—you got any idea what those posts are about?"

The sheriff reached up to scratch at the back of his sun-charred neck and then halted suddenly in his tracks. He held up a hand to silence Parker.

"That," he murmured, eyes darting wildly across the path of cracked earth. "That sound, Wright. Was that a scream?"

After pausing beside the sheriff to strain his ears, the old man raised an eyebrow. "I didn't hear nothin' but my growling stomach. Hall, we've gotta finish this search up."

Sheriff Hall sniffed and laid a hand on his belt. "Never mind me, Wright. I must be going nuts—gettin' too old for this job. Say, remind me after we finish here that I should call my deputy to take over the next shift. Only a minute walking around this place o' yours and my knees are beginning to ache."

The pair of old men walked off again down the path, and a slight chill slipped down the collars of their flannel shirts. Parker reckoned that it would be only weeks, maybe only a few days, before he and Gracie would have to officially close up the ranch for Michigan's snowy winter months.

But if he could, Parker desperately wanted to keep the ranch open. He knew that they needed the money.

As the men neared another turn, a whiff of rotting corn filled Parker's nostrils. The farmer whipped out a ragged handkerchief from his breast pocket. Just as he began to blow his nose, a scream pierced the air, distorted and wavering through the many barricades of corn. Parker turned to Sheriff Hall, eyebrows drawn together as he stuffed away his soiled handkerchief.

Sure enough, they both had heard it.

A hailstorm of realization kicked into the farmer's mind. The rumors were true.

He had been looking forward to dragging himself up to the loft to be mollycoddled by one of Gracie's scalding mugs of whisky and hot cocoa. Sitting in his favorite armchair, a fresh cigar in one hand and a steaming cup in the other, he would want her to tell him that anything he had heard, seen or encountered on their little excursion into the maze was a work of his imagination.

Except, it wasn't.

A third scream, more desperate than the last, pierced the air. As the sheriff turned to him, Parker swallowed. He felt as if the corn leaves were scraping at him, prodding, taunting him. He could not deny his fear any longer.

"What do you reckon that was, Sheriff?"

"Not a what, Parker," Sheriff Hall hissed, lips curling into a determined grin. "A who. Let's go!"

---

JAMES LET out an ear-splitting yelp as Conner lunged at him. He barely swiped the needle across the boy's lips before James ducked under his arm and threw himself out the open door.

James was not even close enough to trip into the shaded stalks. Outstretched fingers raking at the air, he stumbled over a hole in the ground. Tears trembled before his eyelashes as he felt an iron grip dig into his shoulder. He winced as he was wrestled back to the clearing before the shed, cries shooting from his lips.

"If only you'd cooperate, then I wouldn't have to strangle you like this, boy," Conner warbled, pinning James to the ground as he attempted to aim the blackened needle at the boy's lips. James tried again to escape, writhing away from the man's grasp, only to receive a painful needle jab in the shoulder. He tried desperately to kick the rope off his ankles and to work the rope off his wrists.

"Please, stop! Please!" James shrieked, batting Conner's hand away as it came swooping down for a harder stab. The boy's eyes widened as a thin trail of blood slipped down the middle of his palm, the gash opening wider as James spread his fingers.

*I'm gonna die.* Sweat gushed down his neck. *I'm gonna die, I'm gonna die.*

He was about ready to surrender. Reluctantly, he threw his tied hands upward, and let out one final plea for help as Conner brought his hand away from the boy's shoulder.

Then, out of the corner of his eye, James saw the

glimmer of metal slip from Conner's grasp. "Oh, James! My needle! Help me find my needle, boy, my needle ..."

As Conner stooped to search for the needle, James froze.

He took the chance to fill his panting lungs with air. The boy couldn't help but notice the sky. The clouds rolled past so freely, so cleanly.

*Free,* James thought.

Conner kept rambling on about being a runaway, how the maze was his home.

There were the two other children, prisoners in the shed, only feet away from where James was lying in the mud. He pictured their distraught expressions, how their lips were stitched by Conner's dirty needle and thread. It was a fate that would befall James himself if he didn't act soon enough.

"Violet! Come give me a hand." Conner's voice dipped in and out of James's attention. "This kid here isn't of much help. James!"

James's gaze fell from the sky, now tinted dark by gathering storm clouds in the distance. He sat up to find Conner down on his hands and knees, digging furiously amidst a pile of tall grass and dead corn leaves. Violet stepped out of the shadow of the shed and began rummaging through the patch of corn next to James.

"James!" Conner bellowed again. "You made me lose my needle! And my thread, it's gone, too! Git over here. Help me find it, boy!"

Shivering, James pushed himself out of the mud and scooted closer to Violet—but not too close, revolted by her pallid, sewn lips. He recoiled as the girl crawled even closer, and he was just about to shriek when Violet's hand flew out of the leaves and covered James's mouth. She flipped her bangs away from her forehead and stared at him.

Violet's grayish eyes were deader than the color of her cold skin. Her gaze shook James into silence.

After a few strained seconds, Violet slowly uncovered James's mouth, leaving the putrid taste of rotting corn on his tongue. James was close to vomiting when Violet jerked her head forward, emitting a warbled string of words.

His eyes flitted from her to Conner. He was still knee-deep in a clump of grass.

"My needle, my needle ..."

James forced the bile down his throat. Violet tugged at the rope around his ankles and his wrists. But James's attention was fixed on Conner—he heard him calling his name.

"*What?*" he hissed, chills shooting down his spine.

"Oh," Violet croaked, thrusting her chin upward, in the direction of a faraway wall of stalks. "Oh, ow. Ah-oh."

James whipped his gaze back to the girl. "What are you trying to say to me?" he snarled, trying to sound strong, angry. But his voice quaked with every word. He was terrified down to his bones.

*I should do something,* he thought.

Suddenly, she shoved the boy's shoulder. He tumbled away from the patch of corn, and his sliced palm released a surge of blood as it collided with bits of gravel in the mud. Confusion spiked through him. He whirled around just in time to catch a glimpse of Violet in Conner's gnarled grasp.

With one last wild gesture, she barked an order, blood trickling from her lips.

"Go!"

# CHAPTER SEVEN

PARKER WRIGHT FROZE.

He now understood just what sort of a dilemma he was getting himself—and the future of Ramridge Ranch—tangled into.

The old caretaker had been sure that the rumors would be exterminated. By denying the town's accusations, he had denied that his beloved ranch, and all his efforts, could ever be imperfect. To *protect* his perfect vision of Ramridge Ranch, Parker had generated blinding delusions around every bit of the land that he so loved.

After hearing that scream, Parker no longer had the option to fall back on his convictions for comfort.

"Wright!" The sheriff's voice broke the old man out of his daze. He grabbed Parker roughly by the arm. "Wright, there's no time for fiddling about. The fate of a child is in our hands!"

"Indeed," Parker grumbled as the sheriff began tugging him along the kernel-splattered path.

The screams had died out. They were replaced by a gruff, muffled voice—the voice of someone clearly years older. Parker wondered if any neighbors meandering along the road had heard the screams. Another chill scurried down his spine as visions of more articles filled his spinning head.

Parker gritted his teeth and pressed onward by Sheriff Hall's side.

He would ensure that Ramridge Ranch regained its reputation as the county's finest farm in history. They would solve this mystery, even if it meant Ramridge wouldn't be the same glimmering jewel that it once was, before any of this nonsense set foot on his soil.

The screams arose once more.

This time, they were followed by a short whimpering. Parker felt a harsh tug on his elbow, and before he knew it, he was being dragged through the sea of stalks. Rugged leaves stinging his eyes, his temper quaked louder than a hundred of Michigan's crankiest roosters at sunrise.

"Hall!" Parker bellowed, planting his feet deep into the furrowed soil. "Hall! *Where* do you think you're goin'?"

The sheriff paid no heed to the farmer's objection and gave him another tug forward through the heavy streaks of gold and gray. "The screams were coming from this way, Parker. I'm sure of it."

"No!" Parker threw up his hand, breaking his companion's grasp. The sheriff whirled around and stared at him. "This is madness, Hall. Why would the kidnapper, or whoever this halfwit of a man is, go drag some kid into—"

"Think, Parker." The sheriff backed away and swept a hand at their surroundings. "Do you believe that this halfwit of a man would be waiting out on the open path, ready for us to pounce?"

Parker let out a low growl. He wanted to say, *I don't care where this imbecile is planting his darn toes. We're not goin' crashin' through my hard-earned produce to find out!* But he held his tongue and shook his head.

"That's what I thought." The sheriff's lips curled into a knowing smirk. "Come on, old man. Let's put those wits to good use and *catch* this maniac!"

---

JAMES STIFLED a cry as he went tearing through the yellowed foliage.

Blood was flowing in wider arcs down his palm. He was sure that he heard Conner's heavy footsteps pursuing him, and he imagined a hundred threaded needles flying past him like poison-tipped arrows.

But as he chanced a look behind him—once, twice, three times—it occurred to him that his fear was in his imagination, for Conner was nowhere to be seen. The needles and thread were absent from the air, though the biting pain still lingered in his palm.

All that mattered to James was finding a way out of the maze before that kernel-toothed corn-dweller found him. Dashing maddeningly through the stalks all night was better than finding himself in the claws of his captor once again.

If it meant freedom, he would run for days—soiled trousers, bloody hands and all.

But the longer he ran, the stiffer his calves became. His brain throbbed with an oncoming headache. He knew he shouldn't stop. Heck, not even the richest man in the world could pay James to stop. But his vision began to slip, exhaustion pooling within him like molasses.

James soon realized that he couldn't go trekking through the stalks forever. But terror overshadows any other desire. In matters of life and death, terror nudges exhaustion to the brink of oblivion itself if it means even the thinnest chance at survival.

But the boy was on the verge of collapse. And it was only a matter of time before thirst would take its toll. Words ran through his head, doubt laced within each speck of hope.

*The whole sheriff's department will be looking for me.*

"Idiot!" James panted. "I might as well be considered dead to anyone who's dumb enough to be searching for me now! And in a corn maze? A stupid maze, for crying out loud!"

He thought back to when he had lied to his mother about going to Logan's house. *Just for a few hours,* James grumbled in his head. *I'm hopeless.*

Suddenly, James made a complete stop. His thoughts had strayed back to Violet and Harry.

*How long have they been here?* Panic rose in his chest. *How many of these kids did Conner steal? Are we the only ones?*

James resumed trampling through the stalks. It did not matter, he figured, whether Conner had his grasp on two children or twenty. James was free, and James had a mother who needed him home.

All he was concerned with now was finding his way back home, in one piece. Then he would find help for the others.

*If* he could make it back in one piece.

After a few minutes of pushing his way through the stalks, James glanced up at the sky, and a whiff of dread passed through him. Beyond the waves of endless gray, it was evident that the sky had darkened. *What time is it?* he wondered. But it didn't matter—night would soon fall, and he was still alone amongst a sea of decay, a monster at his heels.

Stalks rustled.

James whirled around, hoping it was just the wind. All was silent for a few moments before he spotted a slow-moving shadow. There was a harsh grunt, and the sound of footsteps shuffling across fallen leaves. Terror shot into James like a bullet.

*No.*

He started to bolt, not risking a single glance back.

"It's him! It's him!" a voice roared from behind. Stalks crashed to the earth as James's pursuer advanced. Sweat tumbled down the boy's back, blood pounding through his veins.

*Conner.*

"A path," James said between his gritted teeth. "I need to find a path."

*Conner.*

He forced his legs to propel him farther into the web of shadows, the evening thickening all too fast. The darkness fooled him by obscuring the broken branches, patches of mud and fallen corn cobs that snagged his feet. Nausea crept back up his throat. Exhaustion tugged his vision lower.

*It's him.*

"Keep going," he wheezed, muscles beginning to fail him. "Keep ... going ..."

*It's him.*

The boy's face collided with cool earth. A line of drool slipped across his chin. Blackness enveloped his vision, and he lay quivering beneath the hush of leaves.

A few feet away the mutter of a curse lingered as boots stumbled across gravel. A man let out a croak as he passed. The toe of his boot landed on the boy's outstretched hand which was entirely concealed by shadows. James squeaked but did not awaken.

"Darn mice," the voice growled. "Can't believe it, Sheriff. I'm guessin' it was just one of my goats stranded out here. Bleater escapes on a regular basis. He always goes back to the pen for his breakfast. I shoulda thought of that before. Reckon you'll stay for a good glass of beer after all this foolishness."

There was a long pause, and a rumbling sigh. "I don't know 'bout that, old friend. There was that scream—"

"Jesus, Hall. That was Bleater, for all we know. I'm sorry to have troubled you with this." Another moment of silence, and the snapping of leaves on the path. "It'll only be for five minutes. Give us time to think."

"Well, I suppose ... suppose I don't mind if I do."

Another grunt passed through the stranger's nose, followed by a goat's shrill whine. The crunching of footsteps quickly vanished into the soft whispers of the breeze.

## CHAPTER EIGHT

SHERIFF HALL dug his thumb around his belt and turned to Parker a final time before shuffling out the barn door. His lips creased into a smile, though his gaze was heavy.

Parker blew out a long sigh. "I just don't understand, Hall."

"There's a lot not to understand," the sheriff replied. "Parker, let me tell ya somethin'. We're going to catch this fella whether it takes us a team of two or twenty. You hear?"

Parker couldn't help but scowl. "There will be no need for that. It was the goat, I tell you."

"Parker, there are three goats in your pen."

Parker grunted, squinted past the sheriff's shoulders, and counted. Sighing, he waited for a rambling speech to occur. Sheriff Hall only gathered up his arms across his chest.

After a moment of silence, Parker breathed out a long, guttural breath. "Yes, Hall?"

"Parker, I am not going to wait till tomorrow's cock-crow. I am comin' back with a team as *soon* as possible, and we are going back out there," the sheriff said at last, delivering a heavy pat to the old man's shoulder. "All I want you to do now is get a good night's sleep, my friend."

Parker gave a deep nod, watching with heavy-lidded eyes as the sheriff shuffled his way off the front stoop and into the darkness. The old man waited until the ruckus of the truck's engine was whittled away into nothingness. Still, he lingered in the door frame for a few moments.

An idea was seeding itself into his mind, a revelation working its way into his hands.

"Wish I didn't have to believe all this foolishness," Parker murmured into the silence. He turned back into the barn. Parker took the steps up to the flat by twos and for once was not bothered by the lurching of the old wooden treads beneath his weight.

The odor of stale cider seeped into his lungs as he strode through the door. Gracie was huddled in the corner of the room in the great, patchwork armchair. She snorted awake upon his entry.

"Parker," she coughed, her eyes darting across her husband's expression. "Has the sheriff gone? What happened?"

Parker nodded.

"Well." Gracie languorously pushed herself up from her seat and fumbled for the cane that rested across the mantlepiece. "I suppose we better put this matter to rest for today. It's late."

But Parker strode past her. His boots sent the floorboards clattering like cutlery on a plate as he paced back and forth in the narrow hall, arms diving into every drawer and door in his path.

Gracie waited in the kitchen, until finally her inquisitiveness was piqued to the level of irritability. "Parker," she said, hoping to catch his attention. "Parker, what in the Lord's name are you doing?"

Parker stopped short and whirled around to face his wife.

"Gracie, where's my shotgun?"

---

"PARKER!" Gracie's whispers quaked. "Lord! Parker!"

"Don't worry, Gracie. This is somethin' I just gotta do."

Gracie wiped the sleep from her eyes. "Don't 'don't worry' *me*, old man! Just what are you doing?"

Parker's figure had already disappeared down the hall before she could stop him. After rushing down the stairwell and out into the shadows, he turned back to face the silhouette of his wife in the open window. Her features were shaded in the haze of the kitchen light behind her.

Ignoring her muffled shout from the window, Parker stomped down the weathered path on toward the maze, his thoughts buzzing with the headline of *The Frument Review* and the wails that had echoed through the corn. A few yards down the lawn, he broke into a loping jog. The familiar hush of stalks whipped past his shoulders as he ran.

"I'll make this quick," Parker muttered. "I'll run after him, and I won't stop. If I hear him, I'll shoot. He won't get away. No, he won't get away, not this time."

A moment later, Parker stumbled over a clump of weeds in the dirt path. His old limbs emitted a crackle and a pop, and he and his shotgun were pulled down into the rough caresses of corn leaves. Parker lay there, panting raggedly amidst the stalks, stunned at his own frailty.

An unusual noise in the distance caused him to snap into silence.

The sound of heavy footsteps on wood planks reached Parker's ears, along with the occasional grunt, and muddled ramblings.

Fire shot down Parker's spine as he struggled to lift himself out of the stalks. Pressing his shotgun across his chest, he ventured a few more yards down the path, fumbling toward the noises.

The muttering and shuffling in the distance grew

clearer. Parker slowed his steps further, straining his ears. He encountered a fork in the path, moonlight transforming the arching corn into gateways like the shadows of a cryptic churchyard.

Parker paused in the middle of the fork, listening intently. Fear inched plainly across his face and down to his rattling finger bones.

He took one step forward and halted.

After a moment more of listening, Parker cocked the hammer on his shotgun. He turned left and went stomping into the stalks, where the glow of the moon could no longer reach him.

Unfamiliar voices rose in conflict. Parker pushed harder through the stalks, his movements causing the leaves to smack against him like hail through the wind. The more distinct the voices became, the faster he walked, and the more furious he grew.

Suddenly, Parker Wright wanted more than to reclaim the ranch's dignity.

He wanted revenge.

## CHAPTER NINE

EVERY MUSCLE in Conner's body was inflamed. His blue eyes, ringed with bulging veins, widened at the two trembling morsels before him.

"Did you hear that?" he addressed the children, who were sprawled across the hay-covered floor of the shed. Their attempts to feign sleep had been unsuccessful. "Violet, don't be messin' around with me, you hear? Did you do that? Harry, did you hear that?"

His harsh whispers went unanswered. Conner turned away, tugging at the tails of his beard. He could see nothing but black—the night cloaked the maze as thick as paint, and only the wind-blown hushes of the stalks could give him a sense of security.

But now, there was nothing to ease him. Ever since the crimsons of the evening sky had been sucked over the horizon, the maze was infested with sudden thrashings, sounds worse than dogs trampling wildly through a garden.

Conner could not figure out who, or what, would enter the maze at such an hour.

Staring blindly out into the dark, the thought dawned on Conner that perhaps, just perhaps, it was his James moving restlessly about the corn. James, close enough to be snatched up once more, saved once again.

The idea quickly disintegrated from his mind as Conner turned back to Violet and Harry. They sat upright, straining to hear the distant sounds.

"Well." Conner craned his neck to gaze back into the night. "We've a big day tomorrow. We better get to—"

A harsh beam of light suddenly blinded Conner. He doubled over, then looked up and caught a glimpse of a broad silhouette emerging from the stalks. Quickly, he pressed his back flat against the door frame.

"Violet! Harry!" he shouted, fumbling to push himself away from the frame as the footsteps crunched louder through the corn. He flung one arm over his eyes to shield them from the light while the other arm crashed into a shelf as he made his exit. Jars of thread and bundles of needles rained down on the floor as he escaped into the blackness. "Violet! Harry! Violet!"

In a matter of seconds, there was a cacophony of footsteps.

"Harry!"

Falling glass, grunts, creaks.

"Harry!"

Then silence swept in once more.

By the time the shadow hacked its way through the stalks, Conner and the children had vanished. The flash-light illuminated a hollow, broken-down shack. Slowly, the figure opened the creaky door to find hundreds of needles littering the floorboards of the shack, and a bed of hay, mud and thread pushed beneath a fissured wooden sign.

"DEAD END."

With a low growl, the figure turned back toward the hissing wall of corn and stalked back into the dying night.

# CHAPTER TEN

THE VIOLET SKY brushed through the clouds, moonlight coaxing buds of yellow from their husks. It was quiet. Frost stitched the dirt pathways and dusted James's confused nest of hair.

He shivered uncontrollably and cracked open an eye. Immediately, he felt the presence of a figure crouching over him. He heard breaths—soft, ragged. James blinked heavily, turned onto his side and winced as cut stalks jabbed at his aching muscles.

The frail figure emitted a frantic, sputtering wail of annoyance. Two soiled hands grabbed James, and his muscles screamed as he was shaken back and forth.

"I'm awake! I'm awake!" he snarled, struggling to push the hands away from him. His vision was still bleary, and he was exhausted from a merciless sleep of riotous dreams. Finally, the boy broke himself free and stumbled to his feet.

He flinched at the sight of Violet standing inches away from him.

"Jesus!" he shrieked, staggering backward, eyes transfixed. "What're you doing here? What happened to—"

James quieted as Violet attempted to mime what had happened, gesturing with waving hands, before returning to spitting sounds out of her crudely sewn lips. She tore the hair-clumped tie from her bedraggled mane and chucked it into the stalks. Tears ran from her eyes in streaks as she slumped in the dirt. She began sniffling.

James stood over Violet, unsure of what to say, or what to do. Silently he recounted the whole of the past few days' events. Terror inched up his spine as he revisited the memories. Then, seeing Violet unmoving in the dirt, he threw himself down beside her. He willed himself to ignore the horrid threads that bound her lips as he wrapped an arm around her shoulder.

"Violet." Gently, he lifted her head up from the ground. "Look, I don't care about what happened with Conner. Let's just get out of here. Okay?"

Violet disregarded his words, her sobbing growing more convulsive. Tears pricked James's eyelashes as uncertainty washed through him. He stifled a curse as he thought of how, just hours ago, he had almost ended up in the same predicament as Violet.

Hours ago, Conner had strung a needle with a grimy orange thread, meant just for him.

Straightening himself up, James brushed away the dirt and kernels that stuck to his clothes. A sharp pain in his hand made him stop. The cut in his palm served as a grim reminder that his life could have been changed forever—or ended.

James drew in a solid breath, looked Violet square in the eye, then eyed the crosshatch of thread binding her lips. It seemed frailer than before.

"Violet," he breathed, cautiously lifting his hand. "Do you think ... I could try to ..."

He paused, his hand hovering close to the girl's lips. He could feel her chilled breath on his fingertips. When Violet remained still, James moved his hand closer.

The mingled texture of flesh and fiber brushed against his skin. James felt like his hand was being sliced by the fangs of a scarecrow rather than touched by a young girl's lips. Still, he gently tugged at the thread.

It seemed to glint between his fingers.

"Mm!" Violet's head snapped backward as she emitted a moan. She slapped his hand away from her lips.

"I'm sorry, I'm sorry," James sputtered, clutching his hand back to his chest. "I just—I thought that I could, well, remove it. But it's okay, Violet. It's okay."

A silence laced with gloom, heavier than any the children had felt before, coiled about them. James broke the quiet.

"We have to escape," he murmured, lowering his gaze from the girl's lips. "We have to make a plan—now."

Violet sat cross-legged on the path and adamantly shook her head. James threw his arms up in the air. "Then what do you think we should do? Wait for the psychopath to find us again?"

She shook her head and reached out onto the path. James's patience was tried as she plucked rocks from the earth. They were in danger from a madman. She thought *this* was the time to play with rocks?

But then Violet began clumsily arranging and rearranging a pattern. Finally, she pushed the red tangle of bangs from her face and gazed up at James.

"What?" he snapped. The syllable came too soon— his eyes dropped. The rocks that Violet arranged had been rendered into a single word.

*Harry.*

James slumped to the ground, burying his face in his hands. His thoughts turned back to the image of the curly-haired runt that Conner had introduced to him earlier that night. *I can't believe I forgot about him.*

He let out a long sigh.

"You're saying ..." James stifled a crazed laugh. "You want to find him? You want to go back?"

Violet gave a vigorous nod. James bit his lip, taking in her expression. He gazed at her hard. "Do we have to?"

Violet nodded and emitted a short whimper.

"No," James pouted, shaking his head down at

Harry's name in the dirt. "It's too dangerous. Conner's still with him. Let's just get out of here."

"Mm!" Violet leaned closer to James and raised a quivering fist toward the sky. "*Mm!*"

James's eyes fluttered in annoyance. "*No*, Violet. You're insane. He'll catch us again."

The girl looked like she was about to pitch a fit. Before she could, James clamped his hand over her mouth. His eyes darted over his shoulder, then, carefully, James drew away his hand.

"You have to be quiet, Violet. What if—*he* hears us?" James said, his words trembling. He swallowed. "Look. If we get out of the maze, we can call for help. We can get the police. *They'll* find him. It's too risky for us."

Violet sighed and gave a slow nod. But her stitched lips were still pressed together in resistance. James lifted his head and looked into the forest of corn, avoiding her gaze.

The hushing of stalks in the distance split the quiet. Violet's ears had been programmed to know every slight crackle of leaves and patter on the path. Her lips trembled, and James squeezed his hands into fists.

"Violet," James breathed. "What was that?"

They both kept frozen, listening.

At the next rustle of the stalks Violet jumped up, touching James's arm. He grabbed her hand tightly and ran.

## CHAPTER ELEVEN

Parker slammed the door, and its thunderous rattle shook the apartment.

"Gracie, wake up! Wake up!"

A second later, he was standing in the doorway, eyes bulging, lungs shaking. Parker watched as his wife cracked open a sleepy eye, lips creasing into a frown. Gracie lifted the quilt away from her as if it were spun from sopping hay. Her voice was slurred with sleep. "Is something wrong, Parker?"

"Not in the least!" her husband growled, tossing his shotgun across the top of the chifforobe. "Except that I almost caught a darned—*ghost!*"

"Ghost?" Gracie blinked slowly, digesting his words. "Heavens, Parker. What do you mean, gho—"

"Ghost! Trespasser! Kidnapper!" Each word felt like a knife slash up his throat. Shaking his head, Parker went to the window to squint past the curtains. "Whatever he was, might as well *be* a ghost! He got away! I got as far as that darned old toolshed—and he was gone!"

Gracie watched her husband as he stomped back to the door and began pacing the length of the bed. At last, she gathered up her nighttime shawl, reached for her cane resting at the bedside, and stood.

"Parker, listen to me," she said. Parker halted in his tracks, but kept his gaze glued to the window. "Don't go back out there alone. Give the sheriff another call. Tell him what you did. He should be here with you."

Parker ran a hand across his chin. His eyebrows pressed harshly down as if giving the idea thorough consideration.

"That's just the thing—he said he'd be back with his deputies." At last he grunted, slowly turned from his wife and reached for his shotgun. "You get back to bed."

"Parker!" In a wink, the old woman raised her cane, aiming for her husband's head. She whacked it through the air. Parker dodged the wood by an inch. "No more of this nonsense, you old man! Tell me what's going on."

The farmer was already hobbling back through the hall and down the steps of the loft, shotgun pointed straight as a lance over his shoulder. He ignored his wife's wailing curse and clawed the telephone from the wall the moment his boots clapped down on the floor of the barn.

After dialing the sheriff's number, he pressed the

receiver between his cheek and shoulder and inspected the barrel of the gun.

This time, he would be prepared to shoot.

The sheriff's telephone rang for a minute. And a minute more. Parker kicked hay about the ground, praying for a voice on the other end. Just as he was about to hang up the phone, the ringing cut into silence. Parker felt a burning deep in his lungs.

"Hall!" he shouted into the speaker, his voice rumbling like an avalanche. "Damn you, Hall!"

He slammed the telephone back onto the wall and unclipped the flashlight from his belt. For a moment he stood in silence, listening to his heavy breaths. He would have to do this alone.

He wondered how good it would feel to shoot a round of bullets out into the night.

After clenching and unclenching his hand about his flashlight, shotgun at his shoulder, he found the strength to walk past the open barn doors. The ranch was submerged beneath the velvety sky, the long shadows more alive, and more menacing, than ever. The scent of corn snaked its way up the dirt path, clinging to Parker's clothes, the once cherished smell forming splinters in his nostrils.

He began walking.

*Well, it's a pity the sheriff won't be here,* Parker thought, *to see me kill that psycho in the corn.*

A SECOND SHOT screamed into the night. Conner looked past the tips of the stalks, frozen.

The sound of a third bullet spurred him to frantic action.

"Harry!" he bellowed, spitting a piece of straw onto the ground. "He's back! He's back to get ya!"

The young boy scarcely had a moment to brace himself before Conner's skeletal hand uprooted him from a bed of fallen husks and swung him over his shoulder. They took off through the corn. Leaves sliced at their faces as they passed quickly as a blizzard's breeze.

"But don't you fret," Conner whispered. "I know a safe place for ya, Harry. A perfect disguise. He'll never find ya. I promise ya, Harry, my boy."

Harry began to cry, fat tears rolling down his cheeks and collecting like drool below his chin. A year held in Conner's captivity was more than enough to weaken any hope he had of escape. But Violet's face materialized in his mind—and that boy. James, was it? They had gotten away.

Harry would hold onto that thought as long as he could.

It wasn't over. Not yet.

A low, sonorous shout, rumbling like thunder, echoed through the maze. Conner dropped to the ground, the weight of his stomach smashing the life out of the weeds around them—and Harry's legs.

The boy let out a moan of pain. Conner shifted his

weight closer to the ground, compressing Harry's legs even further. "Shush, boy!"

The air was still, the sky dead as ice. Conner strained his ears, glancing up, around, down, anywhere to reassure himself that the coast was clear. Just as he began to rise, a series of soft, crunching footsteps shook the ground. He collapsed again.

Another shout broke through the air, like the yowl of a hound at the scent of blood. "Who's there?" Heavy footsteps pounded across the entrance of the maze, a light glaring through the stalks. "Don't make me shoot again!"

Beneath Conner, Harry went limp. The man waited until the footsteps faded. When they were gone, he pushed himself up to his knees, leaving the boy laid out across the ground.

"Harry!" Conner hissed, shaking the boy's shoulders. "Harry! Wake up!"

When Conner heard footsteps rustling closer again, he gave up on his attempts to wake the boy. *What a time for him to sleep!* Still, determined, Conner slung Harry's body back across his shoulder and barreled out onto the path. Ignoring the wooden sign that hung above his head, he set to work locating the wooden posts that stood amongst the shadows.

"Aha!" Conner's boot knocked against one of the posts. He immediately dropped Harry to the ground. "Don't you fret, boy. You'll be hidden, Harry. They'll never find ya here."

His hands moved quickly. Soon, a thick bundle of rope bound up Harry's little wrists, and Conner tied the body up against the posts with ease.

"Never," Conner breathed once more. After tightening the knots, he ruffled Harry's weak mop of hair. "Never find ya here."

# CHAPTER TWELVE

A PAIR of shadows cut up the winding, corn-hooded pathways, footsteps pattering like rain against a windshield.

Violet knew the way. She was accustomed to every dead end and crossroads. She wasn't afraid to demonstrate her knowledge by tugging James away from a false turn or yanking him to his feet after he tripped over fallen stalks.

James knew he would have been at the receiving end of her mockery. He stumbled over every jutted root and rock in their path, while Violet skipped over every obstruction, all-knowing, completely agile. How she could navigate the maze before the crack of dawn was beyond James. He was in awe.

Nearing the end of a large curve in the trail, James heard a squeak. He sensed Violet halt in her tracks just in time for him to steer clear of colliding with her. *What now?* He raised his gaze past her shoulders.

A few feet from where they stood, the path crumbled away, making room for tussocks of grass. In the dim light of the moon, James could make out a crooked wooden sign suspended above their heads. Its words were a godsend.

"YOU MADE IT!"

James turned to Violet. As she swept her bangs across her face, James could see the glint of tears blanketing her eyelashes. His chest clenched. Before he knew it his hand had darted out to grab Violet's again.

Leaving the murmurings of leaves and remnants of thread and blood behind them, they walked forward. The sky above them was whole once more.

*We're free.*

A beaming smile grew on James's face. In a moment, fierce, blissful laughter overcame him.

*I can't believe we actually did it.*

Violet smiled, squeezing James's hand.

"Who's there?"

A gunshot smacked fear back into the children. Then another rang out, dark and powerful. James tried to locate the source of the noise, but only shadows rolled on ahead. Then slowly, like the glow of a firefly, a dot of light fluttered over the hill. It disappeared for a few terrorizing seconds, then appeared again.

Bigger, brighter.

"Who's there?" the voice roared again. James felt Violet shudder.

"Don't make me shoot again!"

Despite the stranger's words, another bullet whizzed up into the sky. Not taking a chance, James locked arms with Violet and dove back into the stalks. Pressing her close to the ground, he whispered, "Another psycho—this doesn't look good. As soon as he passes, we'll have to move fast."

Violet stayed silent, her hand squeezing his.

James's lips moved fast in prayer.

It didn't take long for the footsteps to go crashing through the exit, gunshots firing out into the foliage. Then Violet and James jumped up once again. Without a backward glance, they scrambled up the hill toward the barn, their hands clutched together, minds reeling.

*Would the police really be able to help us?* James wasn't so sure. Would they even *believe* him? He tried to imagine how he would sound over the phone, a boy calling about a kidnapper at a corn maze in the dead of night. *And since when did Conner get a gun?*

His mother's face flashed through his thoughts. Suddenly, making an emergency call seemed like nothing compared to facing her.

As he looked up at the barn, James shook the thoughts away. The doors were wide open, the lights out. After throwing a couple glances over their shoulders, the children hurried inside. James located the light switch, and the moment light flooded the space, he found himself face to face with Violet.

Her expression was twisted in terror, and she gestured madly to the outside.

"What is it?" It took James a moment to realize the meaning of her frenzy. "I don't know who that was with the gun, either—another maniac." He shivered, remembering the crack of gunshots through the air. *It couldn't have been Conner.*

Suddenly, an idea occurred to James. His eyes zeroed in on the piles of crates scattered around the barn, some filled with art supplies, gourds, toys, even old baking tins. His stomach gasped with hunger.

"You think there's any ... food here?"

*I'd give anything for mac 'n cheese.*

"Mm!" Violet pointed to the door. Tacked to the wall beside it was the ancient rotary phone. The thought of food dissipated from his mind.

"You're right, Violet. Food later." James shook the taste of pasta from his thoughts and ran to the phone. "Come on."

"Mm! Mm!" Just as James pressed the phone to his ear, Violet knocked his hand from the dial. Surprised, he dropped the phone, and it bounced wildly from the cord, hitting James square in the jaw. He whirled around to face Violet, hand cupping his chin.

"What was *that* for?" James hissed, his jaw numbed

with pain. "God, Violet—I'm just as hungry as you are, okay? Rescuing Harry was *your* idea."

"Mm!" Violet grabbed onto her hair and flailed her arm back to the outside.

Rolling his eyes, James turned back to the phone. "I already told you, Violet. I don't *know* who that was. All I *do* know is that they're dangerous, and because they're dangerous, we need to call the police to help Har—"

Violet tugged James away from the wall and out the door. Now, it was her turn to cover James's mouth as she pointed to the three posts standing before the wall of corn in the distance.

---

THE SOUND of a gunshot rang out, but it did not deter Conner from completing the task at hand.

"Harry, my boy," Conner doted, just as he finished tying the last few knots around the posts. "Violet woulda loved to see this, I reckon."

After patting Harry on his shoulder, he stepped back, pleased to view his handiwork. The boy's body was propped against the center post, his head lolled to the side, and a rope buckled his chest to hold him in place. His arms were outstretched to the posts on either side, wrists tied.

Conner stood there silently for a few moments, rope dripping between his fingers, and contemplated the loss of Violet. An odd mixture of pride and pain swelled up within him.

Conner could not bear to look at the boy any longer. Just as he was about to leave him, a startling shout pierced the silence. Conner flung himself into the shadows, the veins on his forehead wriggling like the madness in his mind.

"Harry!" Conner wheezed.

A series of footsteps came tumbling down the hill in the dark. Brimming with fear, Conner ran back down the path into the maze—but not without whispering a few final words to his masterpiece.

"Don't you worry, Harry! I'll be back!"

With that, he took off into the darkness, into the refuge of corn, through the winding halls of his swaying home.

Until the Ramridge roosters crowed for the dawn, he knew exactly what to do. He had not forgotten the stranger who had gone crashing through the maze just minutes ago. Perhaps, Conner mused, it was another runaway. A *new* runaway.

As far as Conner was concerned, the night was not yet over, not quite done.

# CHAPTER THIRTEEN

JAMES SQUINTED out into the night. Following Violet's shivering gaze, he looked at the shaded entrance sign to the maze, then the shadow below. It could have been a dense clump of corn stalks, but the shadow was hunched and frail.

A figure.

Violet tugged on James's arm again. The boy gulped as they began tiptoeing down the hill.

*A person,* James thought, his gut clenching. *Definitely a person.*

He had a terrible feeling about this.

The closer they got to the maze, the more Violet's hands trembled, nails slicing into James's arm as she tightened her grip. James felt as if he were walking through a tub of gravel, his movements slowing, splintering. Minutes ago, he and Violet had managed to escape the maze. It was absurd that they were approaching it once again.

But James knew they had a good reason.

*That person* .... His breaths cut through his throat like bullets. *Could it be* .... *It* couldn't *be...*

He saw it.

*Harry.*

Violet broke into an insane sprint. James dashed behind her. They skidded to a stop at the maze's entrance. Blackened stalks bowed over their heads, wraith-like, as if coaxing their return.

"No." James almost dropped to the ground at the sight. Beside him, Violet squeaked. Soon, her muddled, hiccup-strewn sobs flooded into the air.

The light of the moon allowed James to make out a sickly figure splayed in the shadows of the stalks. His limbs drooped at wicked angles, as if being melted slowly into the earth. Youthful, coiled hair hung over his face and shifted in the breeze. The light of the fading stars caused his skin to glow.

Rusted needles glinted gold beneath his feet.

"Harry!" James bit back his tears. Violet cupped her hand over her mouth as she approached them. Together, they stared at the limp body, horrified.

Defeated.

"No," James said again, louder this time. Gulping, he slowly touched Harry's chest. He felt something flutter beneath it, something swift and silent. But it was barely there, and he might have been imagining it.

Still, James's eyes widened. He turned to face Violet, whose narrowed gaze was cast down at the needles and rope at their feet. "Violet—I feel something."

He was lying. James was sure that his teeth might just shatter between his words. But looking at Violet's tear-webbed face, and her deadened gaze, he knew he had to tell her *something*.

Something to give her *hope*.

He wasn't sure she would believe him. But Violet stepped forward and placed her hand on Harry's chest.

"He—he might be alive," James repeated.

A tense moment passed. All of a sudden, Violet sprung backward, lips contorting into a confused grin.

"Maybe he just fainted," James continued, and sucked in a trembling breath. "I don't know."

For a moment, he felt a shift within him. Glancing at Violet, then Harry, he felt his insides quaking. An image of Conner's horrid face flashed through his head. He gritted his teeth. James wasn't just fearful, not anymore. Anger, pure hatred, was boiling within him.

Hatred for Conner. Hatred for the maze.

"But we shouldn't take any chances," James muttered, clenching his hands into fists. "Let's get him off of here."

Two pairs of hands moved in a whir. Quickly, they

untied the knots, and Harry's lanky arms slipped from their bondage. Before his body could crumble to the earth, James wrapped his arms around the boy's chest and Violet scooped up his legs. The two of them carried Harry up the hill.

Before reaching the barn, Violet began making frantic mewls, and jutted her chin out to the maze. James slowed his steps and looked up to find her hand pressed against her ear, her little finger and thumb flexed outward.

James squinted at her. *She wants to call the police.* Instead, he spat out a single word.

"Revenge."

Violet made a pained expression.

"Revenge," James enunciated, shaking his head. "*That's* what we want, Violet. It's what we *need*. Just *look* at him." James nodded to Harry's swollen eyes, the thread that bound his lips. "Look what he did to Harry. To *you*." After gently lowering Harry's body to the ground, James began pacing. "Calling the police won't do anything *near* to what we need to do. Are you with me?"

Violet suppressed a moan, but slowly nodded in agreement.

"We have to get back at Conner," he continued, quickening his pacing. "We have to do it so that we won't have to go back into the maze. And we have to do it *fast*."

The thread in Violet's lips tightened as she seemed to contemplate the idea. After bending down to pat Harry's shoulder, she gestured for James to follow her back into the barn. Quickly, they entered the brightened space, and

Violet moved straight for a crate bursting with overused pieces of chalk, pumpkin carving tools and construction paper.

She plucked one of the chalk pieces from the crate and turned back to James. After rattling it around in her fist, she knelt down on the cement floor. With swift motions, she sketched a compass.

"What are you thinking?" James asked, eager. The only materials around the maze were dried corn stalks, stones and dirt. Conner was already immune to it all. What would they do with *directions*? "If we're looking to do damage, I'd say go for something a little more—"

Violet held up her hand, indicating silence. She began sketching something else. James furrowed his brow, teeth grinding as the image slowly came into form.

"Is that a ... *house*?" James squinted through various angles down at the squarish figure. Violet shook her head. "Wait—it's the maze!"

The girl pressed her lips into another caricature of a grin. She began scratching away again at the cement, revealing a series of arrows swarming all around the winding paths she knew so well. James's eyes squinted at the detail.

"Artistic," he monotoned. Violet shrugged. "What does it mean, exactly?"

The girl made a quick motion with her fingers, as if dragging something across an imaginary object that she held. All of a sudden her fingers fluttered upward, as if imitating the flare of the midday sun. She looked up at James.

"Hold on." He narrowed his eyes at the cement, replaying her motions in his head. He darted over to the pile of crates, rummaged around in a couple and dug out a dented matchbox. Smiling, he returned to Violet. "Would this do?"

Violet gave a thumbs-up.

"Perfect." James peeked inside the matchbox. A large wad of matches had been stuffed within. He began walking out the barn doors. "You stay here with Harry. I won't go back into the maze, but if you see anyone else— like another crazy guy with a gun—come get me."

Before James could step out onto the grass, something smacked him on the shoulder. He whirled around as the piece of chalk clattered to the cement. Violet stood up, glaring at him.

"*Really?*" James huffed. "Why'd you throw that at me?"

He stared at the girl. As she stepped out of the barn, a shot of golden light struck her hair, revealing clots of dirt and blood. James bit his lip.

"Fine, you can come." He glanced nervously back outside, then opened the box to shake a clump of matches into his hand. He handed the box to Violet. "But then we'll both have to keep an eye out for Harry."

Violet's lips quivered, as if barely holding back tears. But she nodded firmly and gazed back at Harry's body lying on the chilled grass. James turned to face the frosty landscape.

"Come on."

Violet nodded, and James reached for her hand. This time, they were prepared. They were ready. Conner couldn't hide any longer.

"Let's run."

# CHAPTER FOURTEEN

PARKER WRIGHT WAS RAGING.

Each bullet he fired stoked another surge of adrenaline, of hunger, under his skin. With each corner turned he felt closer to his target. He had to be. He *believed* he was getting closer, closer to revenge, closer to security.

Closer to clearing his ranch's name.

*I know this maze better than any napper, creeper or hobo ever could,* he thought to himself, leaping over a mound of dead corn leaves. *If anyone's gonna catch this fellow, it'll be me.*

He swerved through a few hasty turns of the maze, following the sound of footsteps with the dedication of a bloodhound. He ignored the aching of his limbs. All that was on Parker's mind was the soon-to-be issue of *The Frument Review*, his own face stamped gallantly across the front page, a hero. Now that was something that would finally be worth reading!

*After I'm through with him,* Parker thought, *there won't be nothin' wrong with my maze ever again.*

Parker fired another bullet into the corn. Through the haze, he could have sworn he saw the shadow of a body falter on the path before him. A second later, he lost his footing and fell onto the hard dirt, his shotgun skidding past him.

*Not again.*

Excruciating pain shot up Parker's calf. He let out a ragged curse, righting himself on one knee. After drawing in a few heavy breaths, he squinted down the path, biting his tongue.

Heaving, Parker reached for his shotgun, pushed himself off the ground, and listened, straining to hear the sound of footsteps. There were no sounds but the rustling of the frostbitten husks, and his own disheveled breaths. The figure was out of sight.

He considered resuming the hunt, but then realized that his joints were not as young as they used to be. Hand on his stomach, he inhaled, relishing the taste of winter air on his tongue. He exhaled, and breathed in once more, eyelids fluttering slowly as he let the cool air soothe his nerves.

But an acrid sensation lingered at the tip of that final breath. And a lashing of pain flashed across his chest. He spun about with a hacking, violent cough. All of a sudden, the world around him seemed to go dark.

Black.

"In the name of—" Parker clenched his hands at his throat. His eyes widened with realization. "*Smoke.*"

Fear tumbled down his spine as he looked up.

A thick, spark-dotted fog streamed into the sky. The heads of the corn stalks swayed through the haze as hot, windblown ash cooked the leaves. Parker could hear a distinct crackling over the frayed horizon. His skin prickled in the heat, and he felt a stinging pain as a piece of glowing ash swept down into his shirt, searing his chest before he beat it out.

His eyes fell back to the path, to the route through which his target had retreated. Frantically, he weighed his options and cursed the deity of possibility.

"No," Parker growled, taking a few heavy steps down the path. His fingers hardened around his shotgun. "His tricks won't fool me. He's not getting away from me—not this time, not ever again!"

This thought seemed to be just the motivation Parker needed. In another moment, he was thundering past the stalks, heat beating his skin, shotgun angled up deadlier than a scythe. Sparks and ashes swarmed between his steps. The air within the surrounding walls of corn glowed magma red.

Parker's boots drummed on the path as he ran. He

was a hunter, a predator, a peacekeeper out to serve justice. No smoke up his nose or flames above his head were going to keep him from it.

---

HE FELT the silence before he could hear it.

And out of nowhere, hot wind like a whiff from hell itself burst through the field. Conner drank it up in terror. In no way, shape or form had anything like this ever occurred in his maze. Worse than being unprepared, he was petrified. The stranger who had gone astray would no longer be within his reach. He could not save him.

"But Harry is safe," Conner hissed as he leapt over a ditch. "That's all that matters."

He dashed through blasts of hot and cold, the temperature swaying dramatically as smoke undulated like a serpent along the path. The flames flapped high above Conner's head, wrenching at his clothes. His eyes spilled buckets of tears from the smoke.

He thought of Harry, of the rope that bound him, of his precious needles abandoned beneath the boy's feet. Conner couldn't live without the tools of his trade. He stopped abruptly, momentarily undecided, looked both ways, then barreled back down the path. Back toward Harry, back toward his pride and glory.

It would not be acceptable for him to burn to the ground alone, no—if Conner was going, *every* part of Conner was going. And that meant he had to get his creation.

His Harry.

"My poor boy!" Conner whimpered, "Oh, Violet! Oh, James! I pray you're still in here!"

The further he stumbled down the path, the faster his legs pushed him—and the thicker the smoke became, stabbing at his eyes like the taut corn leaves.

He detected a shadow emerging from the haze, and a gunshot screamed into the distance between them. The air was forced out of Conner's lungs. His eyes rolled back, body trembling in spasms, voice garbling—a hideous sound that chilled even his own conscience. He collapsed to his knees, hand to his heart, certain that he had been shot.

He stayed there for a moment, his hand clutching at his chest. Slowly it occurred to Conner that no warmth had spread across his skin. The only part of his body that truly hurt was his retching throat, which smoke continued to sear.

He had not been shot. He had simply collided with someone.

Conner rose to his feet. A hefty body lay before him covered with a thick film of smoke. He could hear the person's sputtering breaths. Heaving, weeping breaths.

A smirk crept across Conner's lips.

"Ha! Ha!" Conner kicked the stranger's shotgun into the brush and bounded away, determined as ever to claim his own precious quarry. "You lose!"

# CHAPTER FIFTEEN

JAMES WIPED an arm across his forehead. The fire was getting too hot. Just minutes ago, the flames were only little buds upon the tips of the stalks. Now, they had been transformed into hundreds of livid torches.

But, the hotter the better.

"Violet! Hand me a stalk!"

After cleaning the perspiration from her own face, Violet snatched a fistful of matches from the box, ripped a small stalk from the earth, and struck the matches. She shifted the tip of the stalk into the cluster of flaming matches. The fringes of the husk shriveled and fell to her feet. A plume of smoke bubbled to life above her head as the kernels were consumed with fire.

"Thanks," James shouted as Violet passed the stalk, its tassel violently aglow. Before spreading the flame, he stepped back in wonderful shock. "Violet, the fire's huge!"

*Maybe we're making the fire too big,* James thought.

Biting his lip, he glanced back at Violet. "You think anyone has noticed?" he shouted through the crashes of flaming stalks. "Besides the other psycho, I mean?"

Violet lifted an eyebrow and pointed to the barn. The lights were off in the second floor.

"Guess not." James smiled back at her. "If the owners of this place don't even notice what's going on, well, there's no way anyone else has. Start heading around the west side in case Conner tries to escape. I'll finish up here."

Violet flipped the matchbox up in the air, swiftly catching it before sending James a thumbs-up. She bounded around the curve of the field, out of sight in the ash-filled breeze.

James didn't waste a moment getting to work. He scooped up a bunch of matches Violet had left for him and lit up another patch of corn. His insides swelled with excitement as the stalks fell inward and set more ablaze.

He lifted his arm to his nose, nuzzling it in his sleeve as a cloud of smoke ballooned around him. Before reaching for another stalk, James glanced over his shoulder to make sure that Harry had stayed out of the way. There he was, limbs visibly splayed in the light from the barn.

James turned back to his work. But something

stopped him from plucking another stalk. Through the crackling of the flames and the roiling haze, James felt a presence like the teeth of a lion clamped on his neck.

*This is it.*

He dropped the matches to the ground.

"Harry?" a voice bellowed out from the raging inferno. "My boy! Save my boy!"

James's body tensed. It seemed as if a hand had plunged inside him, gripped his sternum and lifted his voice farther than the smoke, stronger than the blood that drenched his palm, than the words, the life, trapped behind Violet's fused lips.

This was what he had been waiting for. He was ready. He would confront him.

And he screamed with fury, with justice—on the inside.

"*Hey!*" James pounded his fist against his chest, teeth glinting wildly. He struggled to gulp down a wave of tears. "If you want Harry, you have to get through me!"

The crunching of frantic footsteps ceased.

Like a figment of the smoke itself, a silhouette crept into view. James narrowed his eyes at the swaying, hunched shoulders. He strained his ears to catch the erratic shuffling of footsteps over the roar of the fire. Even with the overwhelming scent of the smoke, he could smell Conner's stench. And it was burning down his throat like acid.

James remembered when Conner had dragged his

body from the path of the maze. He remembered the rope that had burned against his ankles and wrists. He remembered Violet and Harry's blinking, shadowy eyes. The needle that had missed his own lips.

He remembered why he had come to the maze.

He remembered why he was still here.

"Harry," the voice rumbled out once again. "Harry, is that—"

"You heard me!" James screeched, clawing tears from his cheek and sweat from his temples in a single movement. "I won't say it again, you—you—"

There was nothing else to say.

Conner stood very close to James. Too close. The light of the flames exploded against the whites of his eyes as James turned his attention to the three bare posts. He sucked in a breath, but his teeth were chattering, his thoughts clanging, weeping, like a waterfall of marbles shattering upon a tile floor. He could not move. He could not speak. He could not even breathe.

Conner looked back at him.

And stepped forward.

*This is it,* James thought again, not breaking eye contact with his captor. *He'll get what he deserves. Yes. I will give it to him.*

"James!" Conner called out. He lifted his arms wide, as if expecting a warm embrace. "Oh, my boy, why're ya doin' this?"

*I will hold my ground.* James felt shivers quaking

beneath his flesh but willed his feet to stay frozen to the earth. *This is it. Revenge.*

Conner took another step forward, eyebrows drooping, lips sinking, his whole face contorting as if to mimic a tattered, peeling puppet.

"Oh, James," he purred, "you never told me why you ran away in the first place!"

A halo of flames burst above Conner's head. James's eyes shot upward, and he watched as the entrance sign flared a deadly crimson. But Conner did not seem to notice. He continued taking cautious steps toward the boy, his arms stretching out a bit farther the closer he came.

"I was just like you, once," Conner said. The shadows across his face lifted, revealing a thousand gritty cuts from the corn leaves. His fingers, glowing from the flames, were spindly from years of handling needles and thread. "Stay, James. Stay, and be free. No one can find ya here."

James took a slow step back. The wood from the entrance sign crackled and swung lower from its chains as the fire gnashed through it. Still, Conner pressed forward. With a couple steps more, he was shaking below the sign's flickering frame.

"Don't you like my maze, James?"

Conner's voice, broken with a hacking cough and the patter of flames above his head, was contorted into something less than human. In his shredded clothes, with his beady eyes and the robotic sway of his limbs, he was the living embodiment of a most cryptic scarecrow. Of the artificial.

Of the possessed.

"I was just like you once," Conner cackled, a cloud of ash flooding down over his figure. "Just like—"

With a roar, the sign collapsed upon Conner's head. James jumped, smashing his back against the ground as a torrent of smoke jetted out into the path. Quickly, he crawled backward on his elbows. Then he threw an arm over his nose and pushed himself up. His eyes searched for Conner.

But there was no Conner.

Bunches of flaming stalks had fallen atop the man's limbs, and instead of a man, an enormous bonfire flashed and screamed and belched smoke in the maze's entrance. James could not take his eyes from the wall of blue fire.

The maze was closed.

In a daze, James rose to his feet. The flames still beating in his eyes, his ankles wandering through the haze, he staggered back up the hill to the barn.

Violet darted past the field just in time to catch him stumbling along the path. In another moment, James felt cool skin meeting his own. Locking hands, they stopped where they were, turned back to gaze at the field of fire, and let the dawn break over them.

## CHAPTER SIXTEEN

SHERIFF HALL STEPPED out of his truck with a flask in his hand and a pit in his gut.

"Sheriff!" an elderly voice called out from within the barn. Though a year had passed since the death of her husband, Gracie Wright's voice was still as familiar to him as the ranch itself. "Lovely of you to come again!"

The old man stuffed the bottle under his arm. After grabbing his cane from the car seat, he made his way up the gravel drive to find Gracie hunching in her wheelchair at the barn door. She smiled her old, rickety smile before wheeling outside.

"The children haven't stopped their chattering about you," she gushed. Hall nodded, forcing a smile to his lips. "Well, you know how it goes," Gracie went on. "Thank you for coming again."

"It's my pleasure, Gracie," Sheriff Hall muttered,

looking to the glow of the small fire illuminating his podium. "Really, I don't mind coming down here every once in a while."

The faces of the children broke into smiles as the old man approached, and the chatter fell away into the darkness. The sheriff skipped the greetings and cut right to doing what he was there to do.

"Parker C. Wright was a dear old friend of mine," he began, slowly, deliberately.

The sound of corn stalks swaying in the breeze snuck in between his words like distant music. Soft, and prodding.

"Tonight, I will tell you his story. A story of two men, three children and a sickness, a power found in the twisting depths of the maze that connected them. If this tale is true, no one can say. There is only one man who dares repeat it aloud, and he, unfortunately, was not there when the events were at their utmost height. I'll leave it to you young'uns to decide if I speak the truth."

Sheriff Hall cleared his throat and clasped his hands atop his stomach as he gazed past the crowd of children, past the stalks leaning to and fro. Though he had told the story here at the ranch countless times before, he could never tell it without a certain queasy feeling rising in his gut.

It was as if he could see it, through the bonfire flames, happening before his eyes once again.

"And that is the story, the lore, of Ramridge Ranch," Sheriff Hall finished.

His audience sat silent, young eyes wide with the awe that comes with the endings of all riveting tales. Finally, a small boy sitting on the back bench raised his hand.

"What happened to the kidnapper?" he said.

"We don't know," the sheriff replied, letting out a short breath. "His body was never found."

The audience fell into an uncomfortable silence once again, and the sheriff, unable to stand above the pool of fire and faces much longer, moved to exit the spotlight. But the young boy, determined to find closure, jumped up, his arm waving in the air.

"And what about the kids? What about Violet and Harry? And James?"

Sheriff Hall opened his mouth, as if moved to give the true answer. But after a moment of hesitancy, something in his mind advised him to spare those youthful ears from the truth.

"They went on to live like you all," he said, eyes glued to the field. "They found their mothers, their fathers. They go to school, go to church—they have good lives, bless 'em. Yes, they went on. They got what they wanted. Good lives, good stories. They went on, just like y'all."

He forced his aching shoulders to relax as the young faces filled with smiles.

"Yes," he continued, stepping off the tree stump, eyes

wandering up to the starry night. "Just like you, children."

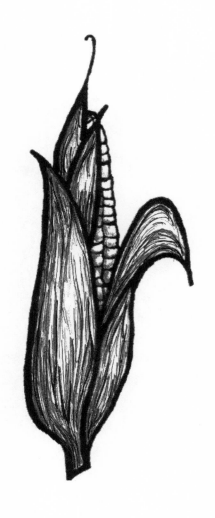

# ACKNOWLEDGMENTS

THANK YOU, MOM AND DAD. Your belief in my writing has a very special place in my heart. Mom, this book would not have become a reality without your long days of networking and publishing research, and your nonstop promotion of my stories. You have been the driving force behind this project. Dad, thank you for shamelessly ripping my book to pieces and helping me stitch the sentences back together into even stronger incarnations. You're an amazing editor. And, of course, I can only thank you for being your silly self—terrifying my cousins and me in a corn maze was just the beginning of the inspiration.

Thank you to Jennifer Walkup and Sarah Monsma, not just for editing my book, but for being passionate about what you do! Your critiques have been very valuable to me. Thank you, Eva Natiello, for your amazing publishing insights, and Lillian Duggan for your impeccable proofreading. Margot Sage-El, you helped me feel like a part of Montclair's author community, even before I became published. Thank you, Shana Adelman, Steve Albin, David Dunham, Tyhree-Shinae Hall, Joyce Hobbs, Michelle Kinnas, Casey LaRosa, Lee Seidenberg, and Michael Starr for all your support!

A special thanks to my beta readers: Jake Bernstein, Grace Carr, Reuven Frye, Max Myers, Mrs. Andrea McLaughlin, Mrs. Anne-Marie Savoie, Noah Savoie, Izzy Kohn-Shepen, Shonita Srinivasan, Sylvie Wurmser, and Serena Wurmser.

## ABOUT THE AUTHOR

KARUNA LIVES IN MONTCLAIR, New Jersey. Her love for writing extends to short fiction and articles on current events. Her writing can be found on her website: http://karunasavoieauthor.com

Karuna has found deep stylistic inspiration for her writing in the works of John Steinbeck. She has enjoyed books in the young adult genre, such as *The Hunger Games Trilogy,* by Suzanne Collins, and *The Leviathan Trilogy*, by Scott Westerfeld. The hardest part about writing, she says, "is reading your months'—or years'—worth of work only to cringe."

When not attending high school, or writing, Karuna enjoys studying languages, indulging in all things (dark) chocolate and listening to Crystal Castles, Arcade Fire and The Strokes.

While she has perfected the art of eating chocolate,

she wishes she could master doing ollies on her skate-board. If you are about town, you might run into her walking her adorable cat, Luna, on a leash!

facebook.com/thehybridageanarchist

instagram.com/thehybridageanarchist

## COMING SOON BY THIS AUTHOR

## THE INNKEEPER: BOOK TWO OF THE LORE OF RAMRIDGE SERIES

THIS PREQUEL to THE LORE OF RAMRIDGE will bring the reader Conner's backstory and describe how he came to be the corn-obsessed kidnapper you met in Book One. Please enjoy a preview of THE INNKEEPER here.

## THE MAZE: BOOK THREE OF THE LORE OF RAMRIDGE SERIES

This sequel to THE LORE OF RAMRIDGE puts the spotlight on Harry, featuring him as the protagonist.

# THE INNKEEPER

## Book Two of The Lore of Ramridge Series

A PREVIEW

The Innkeeper
Book Two of The Lore of Ramridge Series

# CHAPTER ONE

MARI WONDERED IF SHE *would* get diabetes. Everyone —well, not *everyone* said it, but her parents hammered the idea into her head at *least* a thousand times a day. The thing was, Mari didn't care.

Sugar was *so good.*

Absentmindedly, she gobbled the warm cookie she had swiped from the cooling rack just a few minutes ago. Distracted by her eating, all of a sudden, Mari tripped. Her body smacked the ground.

Mud smashed across her nightgown and spattered her face. "I *hate* dresses!" she shouted.

The cookie had slipped from her hand, but she didn't notice. Her belly glowed with energy, like that of a hundred swarming fireflies. She lay still at the base of the hill. The sugar from the cookie heated her gut.

She would do this every day if she could. Mari loved

getting messy—being *free*. What was the point of being young if she had to wear those starch-collared dresses every day? And yank her hair flat with dozens of pins? Mari was already thirteen.

She just needed *fun*.

Mari pushed herself up to her feet. She was in front of the corn field, now. Her gaze locked on the masses of corn stalks, and the night air breathed through her. She looked up. Brushing clumps of mud from her nightgown, Mari stepped toward the wall of whispering stalks, lifted her arm and reached out her hand, fingertips outstretched.

*School's over in a couple of weeks,* she thought. *I mean, I guess that's a good thing.*

Suddenly, everything shifted.

The corn stalks began to tremble, as if magma was baking beneath them, torturing their roots. Suddenly, they stretched away and coiled around each other's stems, interweaving back and up. In another moment, the rows of stalks were tightly braided into a long, moonlit bridge. The bridge reached across to a cloud of mist swelling over the black horizon.

A castle rose out of the sapphire cloud, towering far above her own world.

Mari stepped onto the bridge of stalks. They flexed beneath her stride. In the distance, the castle's winding spires glimmered like stars. Mari grinned. She knew this place.

Sometimes, it was all she wanted to know.

She looked over her shoulder. Her parents' house sat like a rock atop the hill, her bedroom window still pitch-black glass. Mari turned back to face the castle.

The corn field was her escape.

Mari traveled higher along the bridge of stalks, her red hair blazing from the light of the castle's electric-blue stone. A gust of wind tugged her nightgown and flooded the field, shaking the leaves of corn stalks and blades of grass all the way up to the house.

The old shutters rattled. Scraps of paper fluttered out the open kitchen door and across the rickety wooden porch.

The door hinges creaked.

# CHAPTER TWO

A BLAST OF SOOTY AIR BURPED out the truck's exhaust pipe. The tires groaned.

Conner's gaze lolled away from the sign outside his driver's seat window.

"AURUM INN. OPEN YEAR-ROUND."

Conner picked the sleep from his eyes and unbuckled his seatbelt. He stumbled out of his pickup truck.

"Fourth time this trip." He slammed the door behind him. He glared at the truck's worn-out tires. "Piece of junk," he muttered.

He dragged his palms down his face and slouched back against the truck door. Ever since he dropped out of college, the universe had been making his life two degrees more miserable than it had already been. He could hear his dad screaming at him through the cosmos, "I told you so!" or, "You'll never amount to anything!" Something irritating and cliché.

He should have been graduating by now. But here he was.

Conner gazed at his new surroundings. He was on a hill, and glowing waves of corn cradled the driveway that wound up to the inn's sprawling porch. The sound of windchimes rolled around the two-story colonial house, as if drifting from the stained-glass windows.

"More corn." His words dripped with exhaustion. He ran a hand through his short black hair and moved to unearth his suitcase from the bed of the truck. "*Yay.*"

He had driven here with miles and miles of corn fields as scenery. He *thought* that endless horizons of corn was just an Ohio thing.

"Good 'ol Michigan." He lugged the suitcase onto the ground. "Good, little 'ol Mich."

He headed up the porch steps of the inn. Another sign on the door beckoned to him.

"WELCOME AND STAY AWHILE!"

Conner rolled his eyes.

He pushed open the door, and the scent of freshly-baked goods washed into the chilled summer air. His stomach grumbled. Conner hurried into the foyer.

The door shut behind him with the ring of a bell. As he stepped forward, he observed a narrow spiral staircase looping upward into the shadows of the second floor. Mellow rays of light filtered through the stained-glass windows down to the carpet. Conner ran his hand along the wallpaper, patterned with corn husks with thin silver stripes.

The coffee table in the foyer was littered with pamphlets cushioning a clipboard thick with papers. Registration.

"Hello?" Conner called as he flipped through the registration papers, studying the names of recent—or not so recent—guests. No response. He plucked a pen out from his back pocket and stared at it. "Wow," he muttered, recording his name in the last slot. "I actually have a pen."

He returned the pen from where it came, and followed the scent of baked goods, wandering into the kitchen. He looked at the back porch door, the polished cabinets—and the loaf of bread cooling on the table. He slapped a hand onto his stomach. It gurgled.

He did the math.

Four years of eating peanut butter and jelly sandwiches for breakfast, lunch and dinner. The potato chips on the road counted as a vegetable. Conner eyed the bread once again.

He deserved this.

He picked up the loaf, turned it over in his hand and tore a chunk out the bottom. He glanced left and right. *Coast clear*. Conner popped the chunk between his lips. Sweetness soaked his mouth, like butter melting on a corn cob.

"*Yes.*" Still chewing, Conner dug out another chunk. "This is *good*," he sighed, closing his eyes for a moment.

Suddenly, there was a loud bang and the screech of door hinges.

Conner fell backward, stumbling into the table. He dropped the bread. Before he could try to save it, it smashed against the tiled floor. His belly clenched. Conner whirled around to face the kitchen door.

An old woman stood in the doorframe, intently staring at him.

92424486R00071

Made in the USA
Middletown, DE
08 October 2018